THE CHRISTMAS OWL

VIV DREWA

Lavish
Publishing LLC

First Edition

Christmas Owl

2019 Lavish Publishing, LLC

All Rights Reserved

Published in the United States by Lavish Publishing, LLC, Midland, TX

Cover Design by: Victor R. Sosa

Cover Images: CanStock Photo

Paperback Edition

ISBN: 978-1-944985-93-6

www.LavishPublishing.com

Contents

Prologue

WHEN WE HEAR ABOUT WWII, we automatically think of Japan attacking Pearl Harbor, but the war started much earlier in Europe.

The Second World War.

Adolf Hitler invaded Poland 1 September 1939, and the war would drag on for six horrific years until the final Allied defeat of both Nazi Germany and Japan in 1945.

WWII began on September 18, 1931, when Japan invaded Manchuria. This conflict extended to Ethiopia, Poland, Czechoslovakia, China, and other countries. It involved more than 30 countries, which resulted in as many as 85 million dead—both military and civilian. It was a time when the smaller countries in Europe were divided by the Fascists and Nazis.

This conflict involved mostly every part of the world during the years 1939–45. Germany, Italy, and Japan instigated the war against France, Great Britain, the United States, the Soviet Union, and China.

This made World War II the largest, bloodiest war in history.

The U.S. remained neutral during the conflict until the bombing in Pearl Harbor on 7 December 1941. The Japanese also attacked Guam, Wake Island, Midway, and the Philippines. Troops were sent out to aid our allies in the battles against Japan and Nazi Germany.

During this time, Franklin Delano Roosevelt passed away at the beginning of his fourth term as president, and Harry S. Truman became our president.

It is also believed Adolph Hitler committed suicide, which has been up for debate for many years.

Winston Churchill led Britain to victory in WWII.

HistoryNet posted: "World War II summary: The carnage of World War II was unprecedented and brought the world closest to the term "total warfare." On average 27,000 people were killed each day between 1 September 1939, until the formal surrender of Japan on 2 September 1945. Western technological advances had turned upon itself, bringing about the most destructive war in human history. The primary combatants were the Axis nations of Nazi Germany,

Fascist Italy, Imperial Japan, and the Allied nations, Great Britain (and its Commonwealth nations), the Soviet Union, and the United States. Seven days after the suicide of Adolf Hitler, Germany unconditionally surrendered on May 7, 1945. The Japanese would go on to fight for nearly four more months until their surrender on September 2, which was brought on by the U.S. dropping atomic bombs on the Japanese towns of Nagasaki and Hiroshima. Despite winning the war, Britain largely lost much of its empire, which was outlined in the basis of the Atlantic Charter. The war precipitated the revival of the U.S. economy, and by the war's end, the nation would have a gross national product that was nearly greater than all the Allied and Axis powers combined. The USA and USSR emerged from World War II as global superpowers. The fundamentally disparate, one-time allies became engaged in what was to be called the Cold War, which dominated world politics for the latter half of the 20th century."

You can read more at

http://www.historynet.com/world-war-ii

Chapter One

Tom and Mary Roberts pulled into their driveway with the Christmas tree they had just purchased. Their twin six-year-old boys, Billy and Bobby, were excited about getting the tree and house decorated for the holiday. School for the boys felt like it lasted too long, and they wanted it to end so they could go get their Christmas tree.

Tom was a lieutenant in the Army and a tall, handsome man, standing over six feet. His dark hair and green eyes were what caught Mary's attention when they met. She was glad her boys both had their father's characteristics.

Mary was a petite blond with blue eyes and could've been a movie star if she wanted. Tom thought she was the most beautiful woman he had ever seen.

When she was pregnant with the twins, he was worried her five-foot, four-inch body would have problems with the delivery. Luckily, she had one of the best obstetricians in Detroit, and the delivery went better than expected.

Tom always bought the blue spruce on or around the 1st of December, as his father did when he was growing up. Every time he got the tree for his family, he thought back on the fun times he and his two sisters had decorating for Christmas. His dad was the one who put the star on top of the tree, but the kids helped with ornaments.

Their home was a modest two-story on a quiet street in Detroit, Michigan. It had four bedrooms and a full bath on the second floor. The first floor had a family room with a fireplace, a large dining room, and a decent-sized kitchen. Tom and his father, George, put a half bath on the first floor to help Mary when she was pregnant with the twins. Polio may have kept him from being able to fight in the First World War, which he still felt guilty about, but he was determined to be as helpful as he could. Despite his left leg being shorter than his right, he was a very capable man.

As Tom parked in his driveway, his sons practically flew out of the car, waiting for their father to get the tree out of their station wagon. It was always a cold ride home because part of the tree had to stick out of the back window, but that didn't bother anyone.

"Will we be able to put the tinsel on the tree this year, Mom?" Billy asked while Bobby looked expectantly at her.

"I think you two are old enough now," Mary said as she smiled at them. "I think I'll make some hot cocoa when we get inside so we can warm up before we get started."

Both boys said, "Aww," wanting to start decorating right away.

Mary smiled at them and headed for the house. "Come on now. Let Dad get the tree in the house."

Once everyone warmed up on the hot cocoa, Tom went to get the tree in the tree stand. He had to trim it a little so it would stand straight. Then it was ready to decorate.

Mary had gotten the lighted poinsettia garland and ornaments down from their attic the day before. She had to purchase the tinsel since it had to look perfect for her boys' first time decorating.

The ornaments were all in pastel shades of blue, pink, green, and purple, and each had different winter scenes embossed on them in white. Tom didn't think the boys were old enough to hang the bulbs but thought tossing the strings of tinsel would be fine.

Mary had turned on the radio, and Christmas music was playing between news and regular radio programs.

Tom and Mary put the ornaments on the tree as the boys anxiously awaited to toss the tinsel to finish the tree.

"Okay, boys," Tom said. "It's your turn now. Just take a few strands...like this," he said as he showed them how to toss it.

They both nodded their heads, and Billy went to the back of the tree as Bobby stayed at the front.

"Don't worry if you can't get it all the way to the top because that way Mom and I can have a chance."

While the boys did the tinsel under Dad's supervision, Mary started tracking the lighted garland around the fireplace. Once she finished, she reached into a box and took out various holiday decorations, which included a nativity scene that was her grandmother's. The nativity figures were worn and faded but a must for the holidays.

Tom was on leave from the Army until after the holidays. He was a lieutenant, and since the U.S. wasn't involved in the war, he had done mostly desk duty. He did serve in the First World War just as it ended. Tom had just turned eighteen and signed up to serve against the wishes of his parents.

As expected, the boys grew tired of tossing the

tinsel, and Tom and Mary took over. Then everyone sat down to listen to the radio and talk about what they wanted for Christmas.

"I want a Tinkertoy set," Bobby said. "Jimmy has one, and it's a lot of fun."

Billy nodded and said, "I'd like an Erector Set. That way Bobby and I can play with the Tinkertoy and Erector Set and build something really neat!"

"Well, Saturday we're going to Hudson's, and you can tell Santa what you want," Mary said, loving the fact that her boys didn't want a lot, especially since she and Tom were going to surprise them with a new Lionel Train set that would run around the Christmas Tree. They couldn't wait to see the boys' expressions on Christmas morning. Tom also got them each a new bike. He kept them at his sister's house since she only lived a short distance from them. He was able to hide the train set in the attic. They would pick up the Tinkertoy and Erector Set later in the week and hide them in the attic, too.

Mary had gone into the kitchen to finish preparing their dinner. She had meatloaf in the oven and just needed to make the mashed potatoes, green beans, and gravy. She had made a batch of Christmas cookies cut out like their tree and decorated with icing for a late-night snack.

The rest of the week went without incident. Bobby and Billy came home from school Friday and did their homework before going outside to play. Tom was finishing a cup of coffee while watching his boys try to make a snowman and decided to go out to help them. There wasn't enough snow to make one, and the snow was too soft, not packable.

They had a nice house in Detroit, Michigan, that had a decent-sized back yard for the boys to play in. That was one thing they both wanted for when they started their family. He walked up to them and asked what they were doing.

"We want to make a snowman," Billy said. "Will you help us?"

"Sure." Tom started out by showing them how to make the bottom part of the snowman. "Then you make one a little smaller for the middle and an even smaller one for the head. But I don't think this is the best snow to make one. It's too soft!"

Both boys were disappointed, but when they picked up some snow, they found it was just right for snowballs!

They started throwing snowballs at each other, then

got their father. Tom laughed and picked up some snow and joined in their fun.

Mary came out with their camera and wanted to get a picture of them with their masterpiece. She was so proud of her family and loved them all so much. Once the pictures were taken, she told them it was time to come in and have lunch.

"I don't know how you can stay out here!" she said before hurrying back in the door. "It's too cold!"

Mary got in the house and rubbed her arms in an attempt to warm up. She went to the stove to check on the tomato soup and started on the grilled cheese sandwiches. By the time she had them finished, the guys would be in and at the table.

"We couldn't make a snowman, Mom," Billy said as he took his seat at the table. He sat across from his mother, and Bobby sat across from his father.

"Yeah, Dad said the snow isn't the right kind yet," Bobby said as he took his seat.

"Maybe it will be here soon enough." Mary carried the pot of soup to the table and ladled it into all of their bowls.

Tom sat down, rubbing his hands together to warm them; his gloves didn't keep them warm enough.

Mary got the cheese grater out of the drawer and got the brick of cheddar from the fridge. As she unwrapped the cheese, she asked who wanted it on their soup. Surprised all of them did, she started with Tom and then grated some into the boys' bowls. They all knew they had to tell her when to stop or else she'd keep going... or so she said. They knew she was just kidding.

Mary cut the grilled cheese sandwiches in half and placed them on a platter on the table, then sat down to lunch with her boys.

Chapter Two

SUNDAY MORNING, Tom, Mary, and the boys were getting ready to go to church. Bobby and Billy looked handsome in their new outfits, Tom wore his uniform, and Mary wore a lovely flowered dress. They all put on their boots, Sunday coats, and hats and mittens. Mass started at 10 a.m., and it was about a fifteen-minute drive, but with the snowy roads, Tom wanted to leave at 9:30 a.m.

They all got into the station wagon and headed to their church. The boys gazed at the decorated homes, oohing and aahing at them. Tom and Mary only put decorations in their windows for all the holidays.

After church, they headed to Tom's parents' house to visit and have lunch. Tom's parents, George and Martha, always went to the earlier mass so Martha could be home in time to have a nice warm lunch ready for everyone. Mary's parents lived in Arizona, so they would plan on going to see them after Christmas.

Martha had made fried ham steaks, sweet potatoes, corn, and a tossed salad. Everyone sat around the table and said grace before they started passing the food around. For dessert, Martha made her pecan pumpkin pie; she put a large scoop of vanilla ice cream on top, smiling when she saw how big the boys' eyes got.

Once everyone finished, the women collected the dishes and took them into the kitchen. Mary started on the dirty ones while Martha put away the leftovers. The boys went out to play, and the men went into the living room to listen to the radio.

While listening to the radio, the phone rang, and since the women were busy in the kitchen, George got up to answer it. The phone was on a small table just off the living room, and Tom could see his father.

"Hello," George said into the phone. "Yes, he's here. One moment."

He turned to the living room, holding out the phone. "Son, it's for you."

Tom wondered who would call for him there; he hadn't lived there in years.

"Hello?" Tom said, the curiosity obvious in his voice.

"Lieutenant Thomas Roberts?" the voice asked.

"Yes, this is."

"You are required to report to the Selfridge," said the voice he recognized as Lt. Phil Peterson. "The plane is going to leave at fifteen hundred hours."

"What's going on, Phil?"

"I'm not allowed to tell you any more than that, Tom. Sorry."

"I'll be there as soon as I can." He hung up.

His father looked at him with deep lines of concern on his face. "What is it, son?"

"They won't say, but I have to report in." Tom glanced out the window at his boys playing in the front yard and felt his heart break. "I'll let you know as soon as I do."

Reluctantly, he walked into the kitchen where the women were giggling as they did the dishes.

Martha noticed him first. "What's wrong? Who was that on the phone?" she asked, feeling the pull in her gut. He only had two years in his tour, and she prayed he'd never have to go to war. Tears welled up in her eyes.

Mary tensed up before she turned, having the feeling it wasn't good news. She looked at Tom. "No," she whispered just before the tears began to fall.

Tom walked to her and took her in his arms. "I'm

not sure what's going on." He put an arm around his mother. "I have to report in at once, so when I know what's going on, I'll call. I have to leave right away. That's all I know."

George called the boys in; they needed to know. They weren't too happy about coming in, but they always obeyed.

Once they got their snow outfits off, they saw the tears on their mother and grandmother's faces. This brought tears to their own eyes. Their father knelt and wrapped his arms around both.

"I have to leave for a while," Tom said as he backed away enough to look into their eyes.

"You going to war?" Billy asked, his lips trembling.

"We don't want you to go, Daddy," Bobby said with tears running down his face. "Christmas is almost here."

"I don't want to go either, but we talked about this," Tom said, fighting his own tears. "Maybe I'll be back soon, but I won't know until I get there."

The boys sadly nodded their heads that they understood, trying, unsuccessfully, not to cry anymore.

"Now, let's get dressed so your mother can drive me to the airport." Tom stood, not taking his eyes off his boys. "Unless you want to stay here?"

"No. We want to go," they said in unison.

"Okay, then get dressed and give Grandma and Grandpa a hug." Tom turned to Mary. "At least my things are already packed."

She nodded her head and went to help the boys get dressed; Martha followed to give her a hand.

George looked proudly at his son, but a misting of tears covered his eyes. He reached out to Tom, and they hugged.

"I'll be fine, Dad. I'll be home before you know it."

"I pray to God you will, especially for Christmas," George said as he let his son go. "Let us know what's going on."

"I will. I promise." Tom patted his dad on his shoulder and headed to get his own coat. The boys were both dressed, and Mary was getting her coat on when he came into the room. She was trying to be strong for the boys, but when she looked at Tom, tears started again. She had a sick feeling in her heart and didn't want him to go.

Tom hugged his mother and said his goodbyes, promising to call as soon as he could.

Martha held back tears. "God be with you and all the men who will be going with you."

"Thanks, Mom."

He drove to the house and ran in to get his gear. Mary had moved into the driver's seat, and Tom put his gear in the back of the station wagon, then got in the passenger side.

The ride was long and quiet until they got closer to the airport. The boys got excited about seeing the big planes taking off and flying close to the car as they rose into the sky.

"Do you think it's just a standby?" Mary asked, hopeful it was.

"It could be," Tom said, trying to sound optimistic even though they didn't say it was a standby. He knew it had to be something more serious. "Just remember we're not involved in the war."

Mary drove to the first gate, where two armed soldiers were standing. She rolled down her window for her husband to speak.

"I'm Lieutenant Thomas Roberts. I've been called in."

One of the soldiers checked his clipboard and saw his name. "This is your family?"

"Yes, my wife and boys."

"Very well. Go to the next gate," the officer said.

Bobby and Billy were amazed by the soldiers and their guns. The one soldier smiled at them as they drove past.

Farther in, the road was lined with homes on either side. They were all the same style and well taken care of. There were other homes behind those, too.

"Who lives here, Dad?" Billy asked. "Do kids live here, too?"

"These are homes for the soldiers who work here and their families and some who are at war," Tom said as he looked at the passing homes. "Yes, there are probably kids here."

"Can we move here, Dad?" Billy asked.

"Can you get a job here? Then you wouldn't have to leave," Bobby said as they pulled up to the next gate.

Tom nodded at the officer. "Lieutenant Thomas Roberts reporting for duty."

The officer checked his name off his clipboard. "Do you know where to go?"

"Yes," Mary said with a sad smile.

The gate went up, and Mary pulled into the parking area. Then the four of them got out and headed to the office.

"Can we stay outside to look at the planes, Dad?" Bobby asked as the boys looked with awe at the large cargo plane sitting off to the side of the building.

"You can see them from inside," Tom said, "and it's a lot warmer. They might even have hot cocoa!"

Tom led Mary and the boys inside the building, then walked to the desk to let them know he was there. The building was large and portioned off in different areas. The walls were a dirty brown and the floors concrete. There were old chairs with cracked burgundy seats and backs along the one wall.

"Lieutenant Thomas Roberts reporting in," he said to the young soldier sitting behind the desk.

PFC Warren stood up and saluted. Tom saluted back. PFC Warren sat down and checked his paperwork. "You can have a seat in the cafeteria for now. We're waiting on one more officer. Then you'll be leaving."

"Where will we be going?" Tom asked.

"Not at liberty to say, sir," the young private answered.

"Understood." Tom led his family to the cafeteria area.

Chapter Three

TOM MOTIONED for Mary and the boys to go into the cafeteria before him. Mary noticed the walls here were also dirty brown. There was a small counter with a coffee pot and a burner to the left of the door. Some packets of creamer and sugar were on the top with napkins and stirring sticks. She also saw some packets of cocoa, which she knew the boys would love to drink. Mary and the boys went to the counter and mixed a cup of cocoa for both boys. She debated about making herself a cup of coffee; she decided she didn't need her nerves stretched any thinner, so she passed.

Tom walked into the room and smiled when he saw his buddy Mark sitting at a small square table with another man he didn't recognize. Mary and the boys came to his side. "Guess Larry's not here yet," he said, leading his family toward the tables.

"Hey, look what the cat dragged in," Lt. Mark Thurman said as he got up and extended a hand to Tom. Tom shook his hand and grinned. Mark was as tall as Tom but had bright red hair and green eyes.

"You should talk," Tom said as the two men chuckled.

"This is PFC Carl Wisniewski," Mark told Tom.

Tom sat down next to him and shook hands. Carl had blond hair and blue eyes but was under six feet.

"How do you do, sir?" Carl said.

"You don't have to call me sir now, Carl. Tom is fine. This is my wife, Mary, and my boys, Billy and Bobby."

Mark and Carl said hello then sat back down.

"Where's Carol?" Tom asked. "And your kids?"

"Amy has the flu, so they didn't come," Mark said. "Carol was afraid Amy could get worse. Plus, she didn't want anyone else to get sick."

"Know anything about what's going on, Mark?" Tom asked.

"No. They're pretty tight-lipped about everything here. I think some know, but you know how it is. Once we get to the base, they'll fill us in."

Carl sat and listened to the two men talk about the

situation. He was scared, more scared than he had ever been.

Tom notice how tense Carl was. "Your first call to action, Carl?"

"Yeah. Just finished boot camp and was able to come home for the holidays. Well, I was hoping I would anyway."

"Hopefully, this will just be a standby and we'll all be back home soon," Mark replied, hoping it helped the young man feel a little better. But he remembered how he felt as a young soldier and had to fight in the First World War. Luckily, Mark and Tom caught the end of it and made it home in one piece. Mark remembered losing a lot of men even though he was there a brief time.

"You married, Carl?" Tom asked.

"Not yet," Carl answered with a smile. "We were planning on getting married next June."

"That's great!" Mark said. "I've been married twelve years and have a son and daughter. Tom has his twin boys and has been married for what, eight years now?"

"Ten years," Tom said. "Mary and I worried we wouldn't have any children for a while, but then she blessed me with two wonderful boys."

That seemed to settle Carl down a bit. "Yeah, me and Betty want a lot of kids."

Just then, there was a loud noise at the door, and someone shouted, "Ten-hut!"

All three men quickly stood at attention. Mary and the boys jumped, almost spilling what was left of their hot cocoa.

Mark looked toward the door and started laughing. "Asshole."

Carl didn't know the lieutenant at the door, but Tom did and started laughing, too.

Lt. Lawrence Sarna picked up his gear and headed to the table, shaking hands with Tom and Mark. Larry was about two inches taller than them. He was movie-star handsome with dark hair and eyes and that chiseled face women swooned over.

Larry turned to Carl. "I'm Lieutenant Lawrence Sarna," he said as he shook the young soldier's hand. "For now, you can call me Larry."

"PFC Carl Wisniewski," Carl said, shaking hands with Larry.

The four men sat at the table.

"Coffee any good?" Larry asked.

"We should tell you yeah for that stunt." Tom chuckled.

"Have to be sure you're on your toes, men." Larry

laughed. "Sorry to scare you and the boys, Mary. I just couldn't resist."

Mary just nodded her head, and the boys went back to looking out the window. She and Tom knew Larry for quite a few years. When Larry's wife passed from cancer two years ago, Mary went to help Larry's sister with the baby, Larry Jr. He was only two years old when his mother passed. Larry Sr. was inconsolable for a long time. The Army gave him time off to grieve, but Mary didn't think Larry Sr. ever got back to normal.

PFC Warren walked into the room. "It's time to leave now," he said and headed back to his desk. He hated when families came, not because he didn't have one of his own, but the tears tore a hole in his heart. Sometimes he was glad he didn't have a family yet.

Tom walked to the windows where his family stood. He put his arms around Mary and gave her a long kiss and strong hug. When he pulled back, he saw the tears in her eyes. One thing Tom knew was you never said everything will be all right; it was bad luck.

He squatted down and wrapped his arms around his boys and gave them a big hug and kissed their cheeks. "Now, I expect you two to mind your mother while I'm gone."

The boys nodded their heads, tears streaming down

their faces. Tom wrapped his arms around them again, so tempted to say everything would be all right.

He stood and kissed Mary one last time and walked over to the table to get his gear. When he got to the door, he turned and waved to them and followed the other men out.

Chapter Four

THE FOUR MEN were led to the same cargo plane Tom's boys were excited about seeing, the one close to the cafeteria window. He wondered if they stayed in the cafeteria until he left or if Mary decided to leave before she started crying so hard she wouldn't be able to drive. Tom couldn't make himself turn to look and just got on the plane.

There were four other men on the plane, seated on one side, strapped in and ready to go.

The copilot greeted them. "Sergeant Phil Anderson," he said, reaching forward to shake their hands. "You four sit here and fasten yourselves in." He pointed to the one side. The men sat down and did as they were instructed.

Tom noticed several tanks and tons of other armaments loaded in the back of the plane, which told him this was not going to be a standby. The Army wouldn't need this much firepower for standby, and that made his heart sink. Mark and Larry had the same thought going through their heads. Tom, Mark, and Larry looked at each other then turned to Carl, who was white as a ghost. They didn't know Carl had noticed the expressions on their faces, setting the fear of God in him.

Carl didn't mind serving his country; he was proud to be a soldier and serve as his father and grandfather had. His grandfather served his whole life and had made it to two-star General before a massive heart attack took his life. Carl kept that in his mind to try to calm himself down. His father served but decided not to make a career out of it as his father had. Two tours of duty were plenty for him. Carl wondered if he would follow his grandfather's career or his father's.

Carl turned to Tom. "It's worse than we thought, isn't it?"

"It might be," Tom said. "Once we get to the base in England, we'll know for sure. Nobody seems to want to tell us anything yet."

"We're going to England?" Carl asked with wide eyes. "They never even told me that!"

Tom, Mark, and Larry frowned, all nodding their heads.

"Sorry, sport. That's all we know. Why we're going there is still a mystery," Larry said. "We were lucky to get that much from them."

"Do you guys know what's going on?" Mark asked, looking at the four soldiers sitting across from them.

"No, sir," said a handsome soldier with dark brown hair and eyes. "We're as much in the dark as you are. All we know is we're going to the base in England. I'm PFC Paul Madina. This is PFC Bill Edmonds, PFC Raul Sanchez, and PFC Mike Stoltenberg. We're all from Livonia."

Tom couldn't help thinking they were just babies like Carl. He figured they were all probably about twenty. Edmonds was pimply-faced and blond with blue eyes, Sanchez dark hair and green eyes, and Stoltenberg a handsome blond with bright blue eyes.

Tom and his group made their introductions and then started talking about their families and where they were from.

The plane jerked as it started to taxi down the runway. Some of the equipment moved in the back of the plane and caused the eight men to jump. There was a lot more noise as the plane took flight and the equipment moved to the back. Once the plane leveled out, everything settled in the back, and the conversation turned to their mysterious mission.

"Maybe the Brits need our help?" Edmonds said. "Hitler's been running wild in Europe."

"So, we're unofficially in the war?" Carl asked the men sitting across from them. They seemed to know a little more than he and his group did.

"Yeah, I guess so," Edmonds answered. "We have been since March, but they haven't sent too many people over. The Air Force has been there at least that long."

Tom thought for a moment. "The Tigers were sent then, weren't they?"

"Yes, sir," Madina answered. "My brother is with them, so we knew he was going right away."

Carl swallowed hard, considering this new information. "Anyone ever been to England? Or overseas?"

"I've been there once after World War One," Mark said. "Tom, Larry, and I had gone there six years ago. We were part of a team that worked with the allies to see what could be done if another war broke out."

"They expected another war?" Edmonds asked.

"England and France were worried there would be another one but expected it a lot sooner. It didn't happen until 1939, though," Mark answered.

"I was there on vacation a couple of years ago," Edmonds said. "I went with my family."

"The only place I ever went was Hawaii for my

honeymoon," Stoltenberg said. "But I never left the U.S."

"I went to Spain with my parents to visit family that was there," Sanchez said. "Never been anywhere else."

Madina sat there and said, "I've never been anywhere out of the U.S. Traveled around our country though. Now I will be able to say I've been to a foreign country." Madina yawned and looked at his watch. "It's almost twenty-two hundred hours. No wonder I'm tired."

Edmonds nodded. "We all are, and we're going back, so it's only going on seventeen hundred hours in England."

"I hope we get a break before any briefings," Madina said.

Stoltenberg stretched his back. "Well, I'm wide awake. I want to know what's going on."

The other men shook their heads, and some yawned.

Chapter Five

THE PLANE HIT some turbulence several times during the flight, and the equipment moved again.

"I sure hope those tanks are good and secure," Edmonds said, looking wide-eyed at the back of the plane. "When we land, I don't want it coming at us."

The men all chuckled.

"Everything is secure, son," Tom said. "They wouldn't want it to come loose and crush us."

Carl's eyes got wide, and he decided to just sit back and wait for the plane to land. They had quite a few hours left, so some took a nap—at least the ones who could.

The plane started its descent, and the men felt the landing gear drop. They all steadied themselves while the plane made a rather bumpy landing causing everything to shake. The equipment and tanks stayed where they were anchored to the cargo section of the plane.

Once the plane stopped, the men unfastened themselves and stood and stretched. They had gotten up several times during the flight to stretch but quickly sat back down and fastened themselves back into their spots. Now they could stay standing.

They exited the plane and noticed a group of officers approaching them.

"Ten-hut!" Larry said, and all eight of the men stopped and saluted as Major Sylvester "Sly" Rich and Sgt. Ralph Furlong came into view. They saluted the men.

"At ease, gentlemen," the major said. The men stood at attention. "Follow Sergeant Ralph Furlong to stow your gear for now and get some rest. We have a meeting at twenty-two hundred hours. I don't want to waste time."

"Follow me, men," Sgt. Furlong said. He led them to a bunkroom with ten bunk beds on each side. "You can use these beds for now. I'll be back to get you in five hours."

The men saluted, and Furlong left. They all tossed

their gear near a bunk and lay down without taking off their boots. But despite being exhausted, sleep was hard to come by; they were too nervous.

"It sure feels good to be back on solid ground," Sanchez said. "I was sure some of that stuff was going to crush us."

"Yeah, it does." Madina yawned, and the other men started to also. Before long, they had all slipped into a light sleep.

The door swung open, and Sgt. Furlong made sure to slam it to the wall. "All right, ladies. Time to get up."

The eight men jumped up and saluted. They knew it was going to be business from this point on.

"Follow me," Furlong said and led the eight men to a large area. "Lieutenants in the front. The rest of you take seats where you can find them."

There were about thirty-four men in the room, and they took their seats as instructed. The room was large, maybe twenty feet by twenty feet, and the walls were gray just like the floor. Folded metal chairs filled most of the room. A desk, podium, and screen occupied the front. The major, Sgt. Furlong, and two other sergeants stood in the front of the room. All five officers had forlorn looks on their faces.

Major Waters looked them over and began. "Yesterday, at zero seventy fifty-three hours, the Japanese bombed Pearl Harbor. The second attack was zero eighty fifty-five hours. Then they attacked the Philippines, Guam, Wake Island, and Midway."

Shock hit the men in the seats, and low murmurs could be heard throughout the room. The major waited, knowing it was the worst news these men had ever heard.

"We have been notified by President Roosevelt that we will be entering the war. The president announced this to the people of the U.S. at thirteen three zero hours today.

"You may be wondering why you were sent here instead of to the base in Hawaii. It was decided troops were needed here to help with the European conflict. Others were sent to the Hawaiian base to help them fight those bastard Japs."

The major looked at the three lieutenants. "Each of you will be with one of these sergeants and will have your own platoons," he said, turning to the sergeants as he mentioned them. "Tom, you will be with Sergeant James Watchman. Mark, you will be with Sergeant Ralph Furlong. Larry, you'll be with Sergeant Wilbur

Forrest. The rest of you have been assigned to each platoon."

Sgt. Furlong pulled down a map of Germany and grabbed a pointer lying on the desk. "You will be heading to Germany to cover the area around Poland. Most of the area is wooded and has some hills but very few civilians. A helicopter will drop each of you off in three hours, so get with your men and get ready. Okay, men, let's move."

As the men stood and set off to prepare, Sgt. Furlong waved the sergeants and lieutenants over. "Men, I feel I need to inform you these are experimental helicopters. We got the idea from the Germans. We'll be fighting them with their own weapon! These helicopters are very quiet, and this will be to your advantage. Perhaps keep this under your hats for now. These men have enough on their plates. Be certain we'd never send our own out in something that isn't safe."

Chapter Six

THREE HELICOPTERS WERE ready to collect the men and head out to their assigned destinations. It was dark and quiet, giving the mission a more eerie feel than they would have liked. Roberts and Watchman were the last to get on the first helicopter to leave.

Their helicopter set down in an open area and let the men off. Once they were all on the ground, the helicopter departed, returning to base. The men looked to Roberts and Watchman for their orders, all wondering what they were going to be in for now.

Watchman took out a small flashlight and a map. "We're heading south toward the hills on the other side of this copse of trees. Remember the plan, men. If we get separated, we continue south and seek refuge in

Switzerland. I know it's a hell of a trek, but it's our best bet. Stay alert for anything out of the ordinary."

Watchman and Roberts led the men through the dense trees, all on guard, carefully observing their surroundings. They continued on for three miles, carving a path through the thick, overgrown grasses, weaving through the maze of trees and shrubbery.

Roberts heard voices in German and held up a firm fist, signaling the men behind him to halt. Not knowing if they were soldiers or civilians, he lowered his hands and crouched down, the others following his lead. They were on the outskirts of the tree line, so they felt they had enough cover for the time being.

"Williams," Watchman said to the soldier just behind him, "take someone and check it out. I don't want to fire on civilians, but at the same time, I don't want them to warn the German Army we're here."

"Yes, sir," Williams said and took Bowman with him.

Slowly they made their way past Watchman and Roberts and headed toward the voices. Williams motioned for Bowman to go to the left, and he went to the right. Once the men flanked the voices, they saw they were indeed German soldiers, and there were about fifteen sitting around a small fire. They could hear them talk and laugh, but neither understood the language, so it would be difficult to let the Sarge know what they were doing. Farther behind the German soldiers were a couple of large tents, two jeeps with machine guns anchored in the back, and a rather large, foreboding tank. The turret of the tank was pointed right toward where the American soldiers were hiding.

Williams and Bowman quietly headed back to their platoon, turning occasionally to see if any of the German soldiers had seen them.

Williams went to Watchman and Roberts to report. "There are approximately fifteen to twenty soldiers, some sitting around a small fire, the others behind them. They have two armed jeeps and one hell of a big tank, and I think there are three or four men guarding them. Toward the back, there are two good-sized tents that might be for sleeping and cooking or meetings."

Watchman nodded his head. "We need to get to the jeeps and tank before we attack. They have their guns with them, so we need to be as quiet as we can. Roberts, take ten men and go to the left. I'll take the rest and head to the tank and jeeps. Pass down the information. I don't want to make any more noise than we have to."

Roberts picked his men and headed along the tree line to the left of their position. They moved stealthily and were getting into position when they heard an explosion. He spun toward the blast. "Fuck!"

The explosion alerted the German soldiers, and they all ran toward the sound to see who or what had set it off. The last place they set up camp, a bear had set one off and nearly killed three of their men. This time, they set it out farther so they would be safer but put it close enough to make sure they would feel less threatened.

The commander sent six men to investigate, cautious about getting too excited until he knew if it was a group of American or British soldiers.

The six soldiers approached the blast site and could smell cooked meat and blood. The first soldier was never going to be identified by anything other than his dog tags—that was if they hadn't been blown far from the body.

Four other bodies were found; the first two had severe burns, and the others strewn about just looked like they were sleeping in odd positions.

They looked around but didn't see anyone else, so they decided to go back to their commander to let him know what they saw.

German spewed forcibly from the soldier's mouth

as he informed his commander five American soldiers had set off the mine, specifying all were killed instantly.

A small smirk formed on the commander's face, and he barked at them to check the area and walk the perimeter, certain they couldn't have been the only ones.

The soldier turned and led his men to the tree line while the commander took some men to check out the area near the tank and jeeps. Satisfied no American soldiers were in the area of their equipment, he instructed four of his men to plant two mines this time —one near the one that just went off and the other behind the tank in case the remaining American soldiers tried to come up from behind them. He also told them to dispose of the bodies.

Chapter Seven

AFTER WAITING A FEW MINUTES, four of the seven remaining men from Watchman's group made their way back to where they originally were before they separated to flank the German soldiers. They slowly made their way to Roberts' group and were almost shot until one of the men recognized Suarez.

Roberts made his way to where Watchman's men were. "What happened?"

"Sarge stepped on a landmine," Williams said. "He wanted to take the lead. We lost him and four others."

"Fuck!" Roberts said angrily. "We didn't think they'd have those damn things this close to their camp. Damnit!"

"I sent three men to keep an eye on what the Krauts are doing."

Roberts sighed heavily. "Well, hopefully, we'll still be able to—"

Gunfire suddenly rang out from where Watchman and his men met their end. Roberts and the men with him ducked back down into the grass under the trees. It was difficult to tell who was firing at whom, but it continued for what felt like hours. Roberts hung his head and whispered a silent prayer for the men killed and the men who were still alive.

Once the firing stopped, Roberts listened intently for any sign the Germans were coming in their direction. It was quiet, with no sound of voices or movement. He motioned for Williams to take two men and check it out.

Williams pointed to Broderick and Suarez to go with him. As Broderick started forward, his foot caught on a surfacing root, and he lost his balance. He grasped the thin trunk of a young tree to steady himself, causing the branches to move. Williams grabbed his arm, helping him to his feet, and signaled for the men to be still and quiet. Squinting through the hanging branches, he saw them in the distance—a group of German soldiers slowly heading their way.

Suddenly, an owl cried out. *Hoot. Hoot.*

The Germans laughed at the owl and shouted at the

bird. Then they turned back, retreating in the other direction.

Roberts silently sighed.

Williams, Broderick, and Suarez slowly made their way to the end of the tree line to check out the area. Williams carefully raised his head high enough to see if there was any movement in the camp even though it was getting darker. He noticed the Germans did put out the fire, and there were some flashlight beams farther away, most likely where the heavy equipment was.

About ten yards to his left, he heard something move, which made him freeze in place. He had no intention of lowering or turning his head and moved his eyes to the left, hoping to see something. No dice. The movement was out of his range of vision, but he still heard the rustle of tall grass.

Suddenly, Williams felt something sharp hitting his back, and he screamed in pain. He tried to roll over, but the bayonet impaled him to the ground. Before everything went black, he heard the other two men scream.

Roberts and the other men heard the men scream but were unaware of the German soldiers approaching their position. Roberts knew they were close, but he was not sure just how close. He knew Williams and the two men couldn't have gone too far. He motioned for the men to move farther into the copse of trees and spread out. His two snipers, Moran and Grey, had sniper scopes. The scopes mounted on their rifles were fitted with infrared night-vision devices to help see in the dark. Roberts sidled up to Moran and asked to use his scope; Moran handed him his rifle.

Roberts saw four German soldiers carefully approaching the tree line, about fifteen yards from where he and his men were hiding. He knew they were the ones who killed Williams, Broderick, and Suarez. The German soldiers were close together, most likely because of where they found Williams and the other two soldiers. They each shoved their bayonets into the knee-high weeds and grass as they continued to the tree line. Roberts didn't know if he should have the men move back or just hold their positions. He knew any gunfire would bring more German soldiers in their direction.

Roberts saw the German soldiers stop and look to their right. About thirty-five yards down, the trees were rustling as if someone was running through them, moving in the other direction. The one German soldier motioned for his men to head to the far tree line.

Not wasting any time, Roberts handed Moran his gun and signaled for the men to follow him in the opposite direction. They hurried, and as they moved, they heard an owl give out several loud hoots. They smiled and silently thanked the owl for its help.

It was difficult to move through the trees with the tall weeds, and it was nearly dark, the moon hidden behind a heavy blanket of clouds. The copse of trees wasn't very thick at spots, and the moonlight would have been welcomed to the group.

They traveled about fifteen yards when they heard voices, and the men spotted German soldiers combing through the trees ahead of them. Roberts ducked down and rolled, getting the attention of a few men who followed suit.

"Halt!" one of the German soldiers called out.

"Shit. Split up," Roberts whispered to the small group of men with him. He looked back to the rest, their drawn weapons glinting in the Germans' flashlights. He wanted desperately to get their attention, to help them escape with him, but it was too late. If he got caught too, he couldn't come back with help to rescue them.

"You there! Halt!" When the German soldier saw they had stopped, he raised his rifle higher, and three other German soldiers came up beside him.

"Put down your guns!" one of the German soldiers called out in near-perfect English. "Do not move!"

The American soldiers froze and put their guns on

the ground and their hands on their heads. The one German soldier checked out the American soldiers and asked, "Where is your lieutenant?"

He walked in front of each of the men, and nobody wanted to say anything; after all, they really didn't know. The German put his gun at Stoltenberg's throat. "Where is he?"

"I don't know." Stoltenberg swallowed hard against the barrel of the gun. "We heard you coming and ran in different directions."

"So, some of you got away," the German said. "We'll find them."

More German soldiers approached and herded the Americans to the side, keeping them in a tight group while another bound their hands and tied them together. One German soldier collected their guns and put them out of reach of the Americans.

Two of the Germans carefully walked deeper into the trees and, after not seeing anyone, came back to the group.

Roberts sat still, crouched in the tall grasses near a thick tree until the Germans took his men away and it got quiet. "Fuck." He knew he'd have to contact base and let them know what happened. For now, though, he'd stick to the plan decided on if they got separated;

he would continue south for Switzerland and hope there were others who would meet up with him.

Roberts knew it was a good long walk to the border, and after traveling for three hours decided to stop and rest. It was difficult to move and keep his eyes and ears alert for any German soldiers. He asked God to protect his men and guide him safely to the Swiss border to get them aid, then thanked God for the chance to get the help the men needed. He buried himself in the tall weeds surrounded by quite a few pine trees, praying he was hidden enough not to be seen, and closed his eyes, hoping for a little rest.

Before he could get to sleep, he heard something, maybe a twig snap. He lay as still as he could and slowly opened his eyes. There was something moving to his right, and he tried to look while keeping still but couldn't make out what was there. Slowly, the figure moved for him to see—a German soldier.

Tom held his breath. The soldier was only twenty yards from where he was hiding and would easily see him if he made any kind of movement. He whispered a silent prayer as his heart beat harder than it ever had in his life. *This could be it,* he thought.

There was another soldier just behind the first, and both were looking around the area, hoping to find him, closing in on him. Suddenly, a ruckus came from the trees behind the Germans. Tom saw them look at each other, and one silently motioned to the other to follow the noise. They both headed toward the sound.

An owl flew between the trees, diving down as if it were going after a mouse for its dinner.

"Damn bird," one of the German soldiers whispered. "I ought to shoot it!"

"No," the other one answered, again in shockingly good English. "That would give us away! Maybe it's trying to lead us to the American. Did you ever think of that?"

"You're an idiot!" the first one whispered back, shaking his head. "It's just a damn bird! Let's head that way." He pointed to the west. "Might find him there." Both German soldiers left the area as quietly as they first arrived.

Roberts thanked God and decided to try to sleep for an hour or two before continuing south.

Chapter Eight

TOM COULD SMELL the ham baking and decided to get downstairs to the kitchen. He knew Mary was getting things ready for their Christmas dinner. He loved the scalloped potatoes and green bean casserole she made when she baked a ham. Mary also baked an apple pie and pumpkin pie for dessert, which the boys loved more than the dinner.

He walked into the kitchen and saw Mary standing by the sink, peeling potatoes. Tom gently put his arms around her waist, careful not to cause her to cut herself.

"About time you got here," Mary said, leaning into his strong chest. "I wasn't sure you were ever going to get up."

"How could I sleep with that delicious aroma

working its way upstairs." He chuckled and kissed the back of her head. "Need any help?"

"Not right now." She turned and wrapped her arms around his neck. "I got the gifts down from the attic while you boys were sleeping."

Tom frowned. "I'm sorry. I should have gotten up earlier."

"Well, you and the boys were exhausted after playing almost all day in the snow." She smiled and kissed him. "You just relax and either listen to the radio or read your paper. There's coffee if you'd like some. Do you want me to make you breakfast?"

"No, thanks. I'll wait for the boys." Tom gave her a squeeze and another kiss and poured himself a cup of coffee before heading to the living room.

Tom got comfortable in his favorite chair and decided to read the paper first. After a few minutes, he heard the boys getting up and knew the paper would have to wait.

Billy and Bobby hurried down the stairs and stopped to look at the presents under the Christmas tree.

"Wow! Santa was here!" Bobby said as he ran to the tree with Billy right behind him.

"Yeah! Look at the presents!" Billy was just as excited, which always filled Tom and Mary with such joy.

"When can we open them?" the boys said in unison, looking at both of their parents.

"After breakfast," Mary told them. "I'm making French toast."

Bobby pouted. "But that'll take a while."

"Yeah," Billy chimed in.

Tom and Mary went through this last Christmas. They both smiled, and Tom said, "Okay, you can open one small gift while Mom makes breakfast."

Billy and Bobby's eyes lit up, and they dove under the tree, looking for something small with their name on it.

"Wow, look at how big this one is," Bobby exclaimed. "It has both our names on it, too!"

"I wish we already had breakfast." Billy sighed. "It's going to take forever to get to it!"

Mary chuckled from the kitchen as she was getting the French toast made. Tom smiled and shook his head.

"Do you want one of yours, Dad?" Bobby held up a small present.

"No. I think I'll wait for your mom to be able to open hers, too." He folded the newspaper and set it on the coffee table.

"Okay." Billy set Tom's gift back under the tree.

Each boy sat back and started opening their presents.

Bobby's eyes lit up. "I got a Tinkertoy set!" he shouted and opened the container, dumping all the pieces on the carpet.

"I got an Erector Set!" Billy squealed. He, too, opened it to get the pieces out.

Both boys busied themselves with their new presents.

"Breakfast is ready," Mary called from the kitchen.

"Aww," both boys exclaimed in unison. But they knew they would get to open the larger gift once they finished eating.

"Be sure you put the pieces from your presents away," Tom told them.

They quickly put their treasures away and headed to the kitchen.

As soon as they sat at the table, they said grace and started in on breakfast. Dad helped pour the syrup on their French Toast, and Mom put glasses of milk and juice in front of each of their plates.

Tom was glad he was home for Christmas and hoped he'd make it home as long as he could. His boys would grow up fast; he knew that. He wanted as many memories as he could have, especially of the holidays.

Tom heard a chirping-type noise and looked around the kitchen. Then there was a flutter of wings and voices speaking in a foreign tongue. He slowly opened his eyes, realizing he was still hidden within the dark forest.

"That damn bird again," one of the soldiers said. "I should shoot it!"

"And give us away to the Americans? Really?"

"I know. I know. But I swear that bird wants to die!"

The owl had perched itself in a leafless tree about thirty yards from the German soldiers, who were only a couple of feet from where Tom hid.

The two soldiers looked up at the owl. "In some countries, they are predictors of death," the first German soldier said.

"Whatever," the other replied. "Let's get going. I don't think the American is here."

They turned north and walked through the forest, looking for Tom.

Chapter Nine

Tom waited for what felt like hours. He looked at his watch when he felt safe enough to move, and it was going on 10 a.m. He stood up and rubbed his hands together; his gloves were no match for these temperatures. His back was sore, and cold seeped through his uniform, but he couldn't chance even starting a small fire for fear of them finding him. He took several steps back and forth to try to get the kinks out of his legs. Luckily, there were a lot of pines to hide his movements.

When he got out of his hiding place, he noticed the sun upon the horizon. He couldn't believe he slept that long; he only wanted to sleep an hour or two. He was hungry and thirsty, so he opened his backpack, grabbed his rations, and took a bite. Shaking his canteen, he figured it had just enough water for a day or two. He decided to ration it to make it last as long as possible. Maybe there would be a creek with fresh water; it wasn't cold enough for it to be iced over very much.

Tom put his rations away and attached his canteen to his belt. With a long branch, he mixed up the leaves where he slept so they wouldn't give him away.

He thought if he walked for about two hours, he should cover a good amount of ground, if he didn't come face to face with any German soldiers, that is. Or even any civilians, fearing they might turn him in.

The course he plotted was through the pines, and he'd have a break in the trees where he'd have to stop and look to be sure there were no people there. Again, Tom heard rustling up in the trees, and when he looked up, he saw the owl. He grabbed his binoculars from his pack and peered through them, finding the owl perched in a nearby treetop. The owl settled its tawny wings around its snow-white body and focused in on Tom. He was sure it was the same owl—perhaps a barn owl; he could see the intelligence in its wide eyes. The owl kept looking south, and Tom followed its gaze.

"You think I should go that way?"

It peered down at him, gave a chirping sound, and looked south again.

"I'll take that as a yes."

Tom tried to see the mountains from where he was, but there were too many tall trees blocking his view, and he didn't want to walk where it was more open to try to see. He wasn't sure how far he was from the border, but he was hell-bent on getting there. Plus, if he kept moving, he wouldn't feel so cold.

He looked back up to where the owl was sitting and watching him. "Are you coming with me?"

The owl chirped again, and Tom smiled.

He checked his compass and continued his journey south to the Alps at the Swiss border, sure he could make ten miles before needing a break. The beautiful creature flew ahead of him as if it knew Tom would rely on it to get him safely to the border.

Making his way through the thickest part of the trees, he was careful not to brush up against any of the branches so he wouldn't give his location away to any German soldiers who still might be looking for him. He knew the two that were close to him earlier went in a different direction, but that didn't mean there weren't other German soldiers out looking for him.

Stopping every now and again to listen for anything out of the ordinary, Tom looked at his watch. He had been walking for just over thirty minutes, though it felt longer. He pulled out his compass again and saw he was still moving south through the dense trees. He chuckled to himself. That little owl was pretty good.

Tom still couldn't see the mountains, but the area was pretty thick with pines and bare trees. He wasn't hungry; he was thirsty. There wasn't a lot in his canteen, and he decided to wait until he got hungry and ate part of his rations or got unbearably thirsty.

He not only listened for German soldiers, but he also listened for a stream where he could get more water. Tom's concern over running out of water was increasing with each sip, only taking enough to wet his lips and tongue.

The snow dusted the ground only where the pines thinned, allowing the white powder to collect on the fallen leaves. He carefully stepped around the patches of snow, making sure he didn't leave boot impressions for the Germans to see. He spotted some bootprints crossing his path but assumed they were from the Germans who were looking for him.

After an hour of walking, he decided to eat a bit; he knew he'd need a little more water to wash down what he ate and prayed he'd find a water source so he could stop worrying about it. He finished eating, hesitantly took a small sip of water, then got up and headed for the Alps once again. He walked only a short distance before he stopped, listening. He heard voices; they sounded like women. They were coming his way, so he carefully squeezed into a grouping of four pine trees. He stood there as still as humanly possible, trying to breathe as quietly as he could.

Through the branches of the pines, he saw three young women, maybe in their late 20s. He wondered why they would be here; it wouldn't be safe for them with the German soldiers in the area. *God,* he prayed, *please keep them safe. You know what those monsters are capable of.* Tom heard of the women who were raped, some killed, by these men. He knew he wouldn't be able to stand by if any of the women were attacked, even if this meant his life would be over.

The young women laughed and continued walking right past where he hid. He knew the German soldiers were in that area; well, they were earlier. Hopefully, they had moved far enough away. Roberts figured this must have been a shortcut for the women, but to where, he had no idea. He decided to wait until he couldn't hear them and continue on.

His legs ached from waiting as the women leisurely strolled by, but when their voices were almost unde-tectable, he made his move.

His pace was slow, but he wasn't about to quit. He

knew he could do eight miles in two hours, but all the trees and having to stop every now and again to listen slowed him down considerably. Roberts hoped to get closer to the Alps at the border by dark, but he wasn't sure how far they were from his position. All he could do was keep going south and pray for the best.

Chapter Ten

"Mom," Billy called out, "can we go out and make a snowman?"

It had snowed the last three days, and there was good packing snow. Mary wondered when the boys were going to ask about playing outside. She knew what they were going through; she was going through it, too.

"As long as you both dress to stay warm," she said. She wiped her hands on her apron and walked into the foyer to see that they dressed warmly. She couldn't believe how fast they were growing. It felt like yesterday they were just born.

"Where's Bobby?" she asked as Billy pulled on his leggings.

"He went to the bathroom. He always has to pee

after he gets all dressed up and thought he'd go before he started getting his snowsuit on."

Mary chuckled. "Well, that was a good idea!" she said as Bobby came running into the foyer.

"Mom, can you tie the scarf around my mouth for me?" Billy asked. "I still can't get it right so it won't fall off."

"Of course." Mary started tying his scarf. "It's going to get too hot for you if you wait for Bobby, so you can wait outside."

"Find a good spot to make our snowman, Billy! I won't be too much longer."

"Okay!" Billy headed out the door.

Bobby pulled on his boots as a frown formed on his young face. "I wish Dad was here to help us."

"Hopefully, the snow will still be here when he gets home, and you three can make a great big snowman together." She hoped the worry didn't come out. Mary had a bad feeling in her gut and wished it would go away. She was tempted to call George and Martha but didn't want to worry them unnecessarily. Mary always worried when Tom was called to duty, especially when he didn't know any details or where they were sending him. And she never got a call to let her know what was going on or where he was going when he left last week.

Mary went back into the kitchen to finish making

Christmas cookies. She wished she had a daughter to help her, but she'd never have any more children. When the boys were born, the doctor couldn't stop the bleeding and had to remove her cervix. She wondered if Tom would like to adopt; she thought it would be nice to have more children.

Martha was in her kitchen, just staring out the window, not really looking at anything. George walked in and saw his wife, wondering what she was looking at.

"What's out there that has you looking out so hard?" George asked as he peered out the same window.

"Oh, nothing. Just got a bad feeling."

George put his hands on Martha's shoulders. "I know we haven't heard from Tom yet, but I'm sure he's okay."

Martha reached her hands up and put them over his. "I want to go see the boys. I'd like to see Mary, too."

George wouldn't admit he was also worried. He knew he had to be strong for the women and his grandsons if something happened. "Okay. I'll go warm up the car." He went to get his coat, hat, and gloves from the closet.

Martha knew he'd say yes; he loved those boys more than he would admit. She called Mary to let her know they were coming over.

Mary pulled two sheets of cookies from the oven and put in two more. The boys were still young enough to love to decorate them, and she loved that. She knew one day they wouldn't and decided to relish the time she had with them.

George pulled into the driveway and shut off the car. He and Martha got out and went to the side door.

"You go in," George said. "I'm going to help the boys with their snowman. I don't think they'll be able to get the head on."

"Okay." Martha went into the house through the side door. She took off her hat and coat and hung them on the hooks by the door as a sweet scent met her senses, and she followed it into the kitchen. "Christmas cookies! How wonderful! They smell delicious!"

"Thank you, Mom." Mary gave her a hug. "I see Dad found the boys," she said with a light chuckle.

"Yes. He wanted to help them finish their snowman. They did pretty well with the first two parts," Martha said as she looked out the window with Mary and watched for a minute. "I wonder how hard it was for them to get the second part on."

Mary laughed. "It was a sight to behold." She turned to her mother-in-law. "I put on some coffee. Would you like a cup?"

"Only if I can have a cookie!" Martha smiled. Christmas always made her feel like a little girl.

"They're not decorated yet, but yes you can." She got a plate out of the cupboard, put several cookies on it, and set it down on the kitchen table.

Mary turned to go get her coffee, but Martha had already filled two cups and was bringing them to the table. They both liked their coffee black.

The women sat down and looked into each other's eyes. There was no doubt in their minds that they were feeling the same thing. Martha picked up a cookie and took a bite.

"These are delicious, Mary! Even without the icing!"

"Thanks, Mom." A light blush came to her cheeks. "This is one of my grandmother's recipes. Tom and the boys really love them and wish I made them all year round. Even without the icing."

The women chuckled.

"That would ruin Christmas if we did," Martha said.

"They wouldn't be looked forward to if we made them all year round."

Mary smiled. "You're right. I keep my boys happy with chocolate chip, peanut butter, and oatmeal raisin cookies throughout the year."

Just then there was a knock at the front door.

"I wonder who that is," Mary said, feeling dread in her heart. She got up and went to the door and peeked out. She backed up and covered her mouth, letting out an audible gasp.

Martha jumped up, fear making her unsteady on her feet, and tapped on the kitchen window to get George's attention. He looked toward the window and saw the worried look on his wife's face and headed for the side door.

Mary composed herself and opened the door. Tears were already starting to flow when she saw the somber tilt of the officers' eyes.

"I'm Lieutenant Clark Winston, and this is Lieutenant Harvey Carmichael," the taller of the two men said. "May we come in?"

Mary couldn't speak but stood aside to let them in. George and Martha had joined them, fearful of what they would hear.

"Please, sit," George said to the two men.

They sat on the chairs across from the sofa.

Everyone else sat down on the couch, Mary between George and Martha, holding their hands.

"Ma'am," Lt. Winston stated, "we're here to inform you that your husband, Sergeant Thomas Roberts, is MIA."

Mary's eyes opened wide, and she gasped, starting to cry.

"How long has it been?" George asked. Tears filled his eyes, but he tried to be strong for the women. He knew when the boys found out, they'd need him to be strong.

"The last contact with the platoon was two days ago," Lt. Winston said.

Mary was sobbing but asked, "What can you do to find him?"

"Another platoon has been sent to their last location," Lt. Carmichael said. He knew about the situation and didn't want to worry the family any more than they were. The platoon collected all the bodies and had them sent stateside. "They weren't able to locate two soldiers, one being your husband. But they're doing everything they can to find them."

This information didn't calm Mary or Martha. They still might find his body.

"Will they look all over the area?" George asked.

"Yes, sir," Lt. Carmichael and Lt. Wilson said in unison.

"We'll keep you informed on their progress," Lt. Wilson said. Both men stood and wanted to wrap their arms around the women and assure them everything would be all right, but that was against policy. Besides, they knew the outcome could turn out to be otherwise.

George got up and led them to the door. "Thank you," he said as the men exited the house.

The boys noticed the officers walking to their car and wondered if their father was home. They looked at each other and then excitedly ran for the back door. They came in and hurried to get their boots and snowsuits off, then ran into the living room. They both came to an abrupt stop when they saw their mother crying and their grandparents trying to console her.

They hurried to their mother's side. "What's wrong, Mom?" Billy asked as tears began to fill his eyes.

"Is Dad all right?" Bobby asked, the tears running down his face.

Mary gathered them up in a big hug. "Yes, he's fine." She wasn't sure they'd understand the term MIA, so she tried to think of something else to say.

George saw she was struggling and knelt down by

them. "Your dad is okay. They just can't find him right now."

"Doesn't he have a radio?" Billy asked.

Bobby nodded his head, looking at his grandfather.

"Yes, he did, but they can't reach him right now." George pulled the boys close to him. "He might have dropped it and it broke."

"Will he be here for Christmas?" Bobby asked, trying to hold back the tears.

Nobody wanted to make the promise to the boys who both looked at them with hopeful eyes.

"If they find him by then, yes," George said. "If not, he'll probably be home soon after." George still felt like he was lying to them, but it was better than an actual promise.

Billy and Bobby looked at each other and then at their mother.

"We won't open our gifts until he gets home," Billy said, and Bobby nodded in agreement.

Mary felt a hitch in her stomach but brought a smile to her face, even with the tears in her eyes. "You two are so wonderful. When he does get home, we'll celebrate Christmas together, just like we planned."

The boys grinned and felt proud they made their mother smile. "Can we help decorate the cookies?" Bobby asked.

Mary nodded her head and wiped the tears from her eyes. "Yes, you can."

"And I'll help if that's okay with you boys," Martha said.

"Yeah, Grandma." Bobby smiled. "You can help with the harder parts."

Mary and Martha chuckled.

Chapter Eleven

Roberts felt weak with hunger, but his rations were getting low. He knew he had half left and very little water, but he wouldn't be able to continue on if he didn't get anything in his stomach.

He sat down to rest for a little bit and eat something. To his left, in the pine trees, he heard something move. It had to be small because only the lower branches were slightly moving. He took a little of his rations and chewed it slowly as he watched to see if whatever it was would come out. After a few minutes, a rabbit hopped out and looked at him. It wasn't afraid of Roberts and bounced up to him.

"Hey there," Roberts said as he slowly reached down to pet the rabbit. "You'd sure make a good meal, but I can't take the chance of making a fire to cook you."

The rabbit sat next to him, enjoying the petting and not wanting to move. Roberts finished eating and took a small sip of water. "I bet you know where I can get some water," Roberts said as he put what was left of his rations and water away. He stood up, and the rabbit just stayed there.

"I have to get going, little one. I'm not sure how much farther I have to go to reach the border." The rabbit looked up at him as if it understood what he was saying and hopped away, back under the trees. Roberts was beginning to wonder if his lack of food and water was making him see things that weren't real. He shook his head and continued south once more.

The trees were less dense, and this started to worry him. There were still quite a few clusters of pine trees, but they were farther apart now. Roberts decided to walk from pine cluster to pine cluster in case he needed to hide from anyone. He was famished now and thought about the rabbit. He wasn't sure if he could kill it, but he knew he'd have to eat something more than his rations. And water! There had to be a clean stream somewhere.

He made better time but still couldn't see the mountains and walked for two more hours before stopping. He sat near a pine tree cluster, not wanting to eat, but he was starving.

Roberts thought about his family, knowing they must have been worried sick. Nobody could reach him because he didn't have a radio, and he figured the Army must have notified his family. Mary and his mother would be taking it really badly, and the boys were probably crying. How he wished his dream were real— everyone together and happy and the food delicious. He could almost taste it.

He knew Christmas Eve was just a week away, and he prayed harder than he had ever prayed that he'd be home in time to celebrate with his family. Roberts decided to start writing something in case he didn't make it.

17 Dec 1941

In case I don't make it, I just wanted everyone to know that I was thinking of them the whole time I was trying to get to the Swiss border.

I had to eat a little of my rations and make my water

last as long as it could. How I wish I could have found a brook to get some water.

There was a rabbit by me earlier, but unfortunately, I don't think I could have killed and eaten it. Plus, making a fire would attract the Germans to my location.

I'm not sure exactly where I am right now. Thank God I have my compass; that's what's helping me find my way. Oh, and a little owl. It feels like it's guiding me south and had distracted the German soldiers at one point to turn them away from us. Well, until a group of them found us. I was able to run into the trees and disappear. I've been praying the men who were captured will be found soon.

It's cold, and again I can't make a fire to warm myself. I'm just hoping I get to the border soon.

I love you all.

Tom/Dad

Roberts tucked the note in his backpack and bowed his head, praying he'd get to the border soon and that his family didn't give up hope that he was all right.

After a couple of minutes, he got up and started walking again. Dusk was all around him, but he didn't want to stop for the night just yet. He slowed, listening and scanning the area, glad there were no signs of the enemy.

He heard fluttering in the trees and looked up to see his little owl friend. "You're still with me?" He chuckled. "Wish you could tell me how far the border is."

The owl gazed down at him and looked in the direction Roberts was going. He still didn't see any mountains, but that didn't stop him. "I'm going to walk a little longer then take a break. I don't like walking in the dark."

After walking for two hours, it had become nearly black, and he decided to rest. The owl chirped at him, and he tried to understand what he was trying to tell him.

"I just need to sit for a minute," Roberts told the owl. "Looks like the heavy clouds are moving away. I'm going to see how well the moon lights my way now."

The owl looked down at him, and he could swear it nodded back. Roberts was getting worried; his food and water situation and the cold were starting to affect his mind. "Maybe you're my Christmas miracle?" He smiled at the owl. It only chirped and looked south again. Roberts didn't want to get up just yet, but it was colder when he stopped, so he continued on.

The moon gave just enough light to help him see in

the dark, allowing him to walk for hours, taking short breaks only when necessary. Tom looked up, taking in the beautiful star-filled sky, noticing familiar constellations surrounded by more stars than he ever saw at home because of the streetlights and business lights.

Straight ahead, he thought he saw more trees on the way south, but they were awfully thick. He hesitated, wondering what was ahead of him. The owl chirped, and when Roberts looked at it, it turned its attention toward what lay ahead. Roberts didn't know if this was a warning or not because the owl looked anxious…if owls could look anxious.

"I hope you're telling me it's safe," Roberts whispered. He was still watching for night patrols and worked at making little noise. He inched closer to an opening in the trees and saw he had finally made it to the Alps. Now he would have to find a way around or over them. He breathed a sigh of relief being so close to the Swiss border—so close to safety.

The owl flew to a large bush and sat there until Roberts came closer.

"What have we got here?" Roberts questioned, looking at the owl and the side of the mountain. He was hesitant about getting too close, thinking there might be night patrols nearby. The owl seemed to be wanting him to come closer and flapped his wings to get Roberts' attention. Roberts looked at the owl, trying to understand what it was saying to him. He could swear the owl was frustrated. It flew off the bush and then behind it before disappearing. Roberts moved closer, and he saw a tunnel. *That must be where the owl went*, he thought and decided to follow.

Chapter Twelve

THE WARMTH in the tunnel was a welcomed relief from the cold Roberts had been battling as he made his way to the mountain. He carefully made his way farther into the tunnel, having to bend quite a bit to be able to walk through it. Hopefully, it would get bigger as he pushed on.

He heard a voice and stopped.

"Hello, little owl," the voice said in German. "What have you been up to?"

Roberts slowly pulled his gun out and continued to listen.

"Have you brought someone to me?" the German asked.

Roberts slowly made his way into the tunnel and

saw it opened into a larger cave. He accidentally kicked some pebbles while shuffling his feet to get through.

The German stopped talking and listened. He asked who was there in his German language and waited a few seconds.

"Who is there?" he asked in English. "I'm not a threat to you, soldier. I'm wounded."

Roberts poked his head into the larger cave and saw the man lying on the floor to the right of the opening he was standing in. He made his way in with his gun still drawn.

The German smiled and noticed Roberts' rank. "Lieutenant, you don't need your gun. I have been out of bullets for over a week. Come in and get warm. I know you must be freezing."

After looking around the larger cave and studying the German, he decided to holster his gun. A noise on the left side of the opening caused Roberts to start.

The German laughed. "That is my friend, the owl. He helped me find this place."

Roberts breathed a sigh of relief. "He led me here, also. How long have you been here?"

"I have lost track of time in here. What date is today?" the German wondered.

"Judging by the night's sky, it's now the eighteenth

of December," Roberts said. He moved to the left side of the opening and sat against the cave wall, graciously welcoming the heat, wondering how it was this warm in there.

"Then I have been here eleven days," he responded, nodding his head as if thinking about something. Roberts wondered if it was his family and the holiday or if someone was going to find him soon. "My name is Axel Wechsler. If we are going to be here for a while, it might be nice to know who we are with."

"Thomas Roberts," he stated, still not very comfortable with this man.

Wechsler adjusted his position and looked over at Roberts. "You can relax, Thomas. My group has moved far from here by now and have decided I was among the dead...even though they have no proof. Some of those men are dolts! They do as little as possible, and by now, my family thinks I'm dead."

"I'm sorry." Roberts was sincere. "My family must have been notified that I'm missing, and they're probably worried sick."

"I am sorry for you." Wechsler leaned forward. "Are you hungry?"

Roberts' stomach growled, and he was starting to feel a connection to the man but was still wary. "Yes.

As of the last time I ate, my rations are almost gone. I have maybe one small meal left at most, and my water is gone. I was hoping to find a stream somewhere to at least get some water."

Wechsler nodded his head. "Well, my friend, before I got worse, my little owl friend showed me where there is some fresh water right in this cave. I always had water, and once in a while, a rabbit or squirrel would make it in here so I could eat a little."

Roberts had an odd look on his face.

"I did not eat it raw, my friend. I would build a small fire and cook it." He laughed. "There is some type of draw up there." He gestured to the high, pointed ceiling of the large cave. "All the smoke would go through there. I was hoping someone would see it and find me."

"Well, I wouldn't have found you without that owl. Lucky for both of us, I suppose." He reached for his canteen. "I'd like to get that water if I could."

Wechsler nodded. "Here is my canteen. It does not look like it, but there is a space between the wall and that rock." He pointed to a large boulder. "Squeeze in there and go four meters to find freshwater. It is delicious!"

Roberts got up and took Wechsler's canteen and went to the bolder. There was just enough room for him to get through. He could hear the water splashing down into what he thought was a stream. As he got closer, he smiled. *Thank you, Lord!* After filling the containers, he made his way back to the larger cave. He handed the German his canteen and sat back down in his previous spot.

"What do you use to make the fire?" Roberts asked.

"My little owl brings me twigs. I have a lighter." Wechsler smiled. "I swear he knew I needed help. I just wish he could have brought my troops before they moved away."

"That's how I felt." Roberts finally smiled. "He helped me get here, and if anything, I'm grateful for the warmth."

"Ah, yes," Wechsler said. "I was, too. When I got here, I passed out. I knew I was hit, but I was not sure how badly."

"Let me look at your wound," Roberts offered. "I have some first aid supplies."

"Gut. Then we will eat." Wechsler positioned himself so Roberts could examine him.

Roberts grabbed his pack and walked over to him. He pulled his shirt up and saw he was hit on the right side. The rag Roberts removed was solid blood, and the wound looked like it stopped bleeding. He took some antibiotic powder and sprinkled it on the wound, applied fresh gauze, and secured it with tape. Wechsler didn't stir or make a noise.

"That doesn't hurt?" Roberts asked.

"Just a little bit now," Wechsler replied. "When I first got hit, I felt like I was dying. I never had pain that bad."

"It doesn't look infected, and the bleeding seems to have stopped. For as long as we have enough supplies, I'll change the gauze twice a day so it doesn't get infected." Roberts sat next to his new comrade. Wechsler looked worn down, and Roberts wondered when he had last eaten.

"I have some rabbit in my pack. The little owl brought it to me yesterday evening." Wechsler reached into his bag. "It should still be good."

Roberts took it from him and sniffed it. "Doesn't smell spoiled. I think we can eat it." He looked around for something to make the fire. He noticed a pile of twigs near where the German had made other fires, figuring the owl had gone out to get them. He piled them on the burn mark and used Wechsler's lighter to get the fire started.

As he was preparing the fire, he wondered if anyone would believe him that an owl had brought not only him but a German officer here to be safe. He was almost having a hard time believing it himself. If it wasn't for the fact that he saw it with his own eyes, he would have thought he was losing his mind.

Wechsler handed him two long, thin branches to spear the meat. Roberts sat there cooking the meat and looking forward to getting something in his stomach.

Chapter Thirteen

"Do not eat too fast, Thomas." Wechsler chuckled. "I know you are hungry, but it is still very hot."

Roberts looked at him, wondering how he knew he was going to take a bite. He smiled and held the stick with the rabbit meat and started blowing on it.

"So, Thomas, what did you do before the Army?" Wechsler asked as he blew on his meat.

"I was an accountant," Roberts answered and tested the meat with his fingers. It was cooling off, so he took a bite. The meat was still a bit hot, but he could eat it with no problem.

Wechsler took a bite of his. "I just wish we had some seasoning," he said with a laugh.

Roberts nodded his head and swallowed his first bite. "It's just right for me."

They finished the rabbit meat and sat back.

Roberts felt like he had eaten a feast. "What did you do before you joined up?"

"I, too, was an accountant," Wechsler told him. "I worked for my family business. My grandfather started it in Stuttgart in 1889."

"That's admirable. I work for a firm in Detroit, Michigan. My grandfather was a career officer. My dad was a lawyer before he retired."

"So, you are the first to go into accounting then?"

"No. My brother works with me." Roberts took a sip of his water. It tasted heavenly. "He's two years older and got the job first. Then I was able to start working there."

"What about your family? Wife? Children?"

"They're waiting to hear from me." Despair made Roberts' chest feel heavy like a weight was on it. "I haven't been able to connect with the Army to let them know I'm still alive. My wife is Mary, and I have twin boys, Billy and Bobby. They're only six years old. I promised them I'd be home for Christmas, but it doesn't look like I'll make it."

"You never know, Thomas." Wechsler smiled. "We might both get a Christmas miracle!"

Roberts smiled back. "Yes, we could. What about yours? You mentioned having a family earlier."

"Yes, and I'm sick at the thought of them grieving for me, thinking I'm dead—all because nobody has sent a recon group out looking for me." Wechsler paused, and Roberts figured he was thinking about his family. "My wife is Hannah, and I have three children—two boys, Ansel, who is ten, and Deidrick, who is six, and my daughter, Sofia, is one. She wasn't planned, but Hannah was happy to have a daughter."

Roberts nodded his head. "Mary wanted a large family, but she had complications with the twins and can't have any more children. I know she would have been happy to have a little girl, too."

"I am so sorry for you." Wechsler shook his head. "You never know what could happen, though, so don't give up."

Just then, the little owl flew into the cave, startling Roberts; the kind bird hadn't been there since he led him to the cave.

Wechsler let out a hardy laugh. "You will get used to him. It took me a few times to not get scared to death!"

"Hey, little owl." Roberts smiled at him. "Thank you for bringing me here."

The little owl looked down at him and chirped before flying over to Wechsler to check on him. Satisfied the men were doing well, he chittered and flew out of the cave.

The two men spent the next five days talking about their families and accounting. Roberts was glad Wechsler was an accountant because, besides their families, they had something to talk about.

The little owl would come in with a rabbit or squirrel for the men to eat, and Roberts finally stopped jumping every time it came in. Wechsler looked like he was getting weaker even though he had the meat. Roberts wondered if he had a serious infection setting in his wound and spreading throughout his body.

"How are you feeling, Axel?" Roberts was told to call him by his first name as it didn't feel so formal. Besides, they didn't know how long they would be there.

"Just a little tired." Wechsler took a drink of water. "I am not a very religious man, but I have been praying since I have been here."

"I pray every day. We go to church every Sunday and holyday."

"Catholic?" Wechsler asked, wincing as he shifted himself, the pain evident on his face.

"Let me check that for you." Roberts made his way to Wechsler to check on his wound. "Yes, we are Catholic." He was out of sterile gauze and antibiotic powder to treat him. He pulled the gauze off the wound, and it didn't look infected, but that didn't mean an infection wasn't coursing through his body. He reached over and felt Wechsler's forehead; he was cool. Perhaps the cold rocks were helping keep the fever down, but they wouldn't do anything for an infection.

"Do not worry, my friend," Wechsler told him. "I have a feeling we are going to be found soon."

"I sure hope so, Axel." Roberts knew if they didn't find them, Axel would surely die. He sat down next to him and pulled out a picture. "This is my family."

Axel took the photo and looked at it, nodding. "Handsome family. Your sons look a lot like you." He reached into his pocket and took out his picture of his family and handed it to Roberts.

"Lovely, Axel. Your boys look just like you, and your daughter looks like your wife."

"Thank you," Wechsler said with sadness in his eyes. "What day is today?"

"It's December twenty-third. Tomorrow is Christmas Eve." Roberts mirrored his friend's sorrow, knowing he wouldn't be with his family.

There was a commotion outside the cave, and

Roberts heard English-speaking voices. His heart jumped in his chest; they found them.

The little owl flew into the cave, and a soldier followed behind, his rifle drawn. He looked around and saw Roberts and then the German soldier. He recoiled a little from the stench.

Roberts sighed. "You don't know how glad I am to see you boys. I'm Lieutenant Thomas Roberts, and I've been here for five days. He's been here for sixteen," Roberts told them, pointing to the German soldier.

"I'm Lieutenant Will Weston. You won't believe it when I tell you this little owl brought us here."

"Oh, yes, I would! He brought us here too," Roberts said and nodded his head toward his friend.

"We found seven bodies," the young soldier said, his face a bit ashen. "We'll be transporting them back to base. Are you wounded?"

"No, I'm fine, but my friend there may have an infection. His wound looks good, but he's been getting weaker." He spotted two other soldiers enter the cave behind Lt. Weston. One of them quickly tended to the German soldier, kneeling to examine him.

Roberts began gathering his supplies from the rocky cave floor, loading them in his pack. "Lieutenant, our other men—do you have any intel on the surviving soldiers in my group and the two additional platoons sent on this mission?"

Lt. Weston smiled and gave a slight nod. "All are accounted for. The other two platoons suffered only minimal injuries, and just yesterday, we were able to rescue those in your group taken hostage. There were a few injuries in the process, but I'm happy to report there were no casualties."

Roberts sighed. "Praise God. That's great news. Thank you."

"Thank you, sir—all of you."

The soldier checking on the German approached. "Lieutenant, this...this man has been dead for a long time, a week to ten days at least."

Roberts stood up. "What? Can't be. I was just talking with him!" He walked over and saw that his friend had indeed been dead for quite a while. "I don't understand. His name is Axel Wechsler. His wife is Hannah, he has three children, and..." He couldn't finish his sentence and turned to the three soldiers.

"We'll get him, too, sir," Lt. Weston told him, putting a hand on his shoulder.

They left the cave, but Roberts turned to look at his friend one last time. His family wasn't going to get good news this Christmas.

When they left the cave, the lieutenant from the recovery team told his radioman to let base know that they found Lt. Thomas Roberts alive and well.

Chapter Fourteen

ROBERTS WAS FLOWN to the base in Germany and checked over by the doctor. As he was being examined, he began to worry he wouldn't make it home in time. Tomorrow was Christmas Eve, and he was hoping he'd be able to surprise them.

"You have lost quite a bit of weight but don't seem dehydrated," Dr. Walters said when he finished examining Roberts. "I'm just a little concerned about what Lieutenant Weston mentioned. He said you weren't alone?"

"I can't explain it, doc," Roberts said. "I was talking to the German. His name was Axel Wechsler."

"Lieutenant Weston brought him back here and had the British notify the Germans they found his remains. He will be sent home to his family. His name was indeed Lieutenant Axel Wechsler. You must have looked through his papers when you were there."

"But he told me about his wife and children. He even told me their names," Roberts said, worried and confused.

"He had a picture of them with their names on the back." Dr. Walters was concerned about Roberts' mental health. "After the men told you he was dead, did you see him that way, or was he still talking to you?"

"No. I knew he was gone." Roberts pictured the lovely family from the photo, the thought of them receiving the devastating news causing an ache in his chest.

"Well, I think it might have been a coping mechanism. You were alone for a long time, and Lieutenant Wechsler's body became animated in your mind to give you someone to talk to."

"So, does that mean I can go home?" Roberts almost pleaded.

Dr. Walters nodded. "I do want you to follow up with a psychiatrist when you get home. I don't think there's a problem, but I'd feel better if you spoke to someone who specializes in this."

Roberts had tears in his eyes. "I promise. I just want to be home for Christmas Eve."

"I'll sign the release, and you can go be with your family."

"Thank you so much, doc." Tears ran down his face, and his heart soared. He wanted to get back to base to clean up and pack.

Martha and George knew Mary and the boys weren't going to celebrate until Tom got home, but they decided to go to midnight mass with them.

They were sitting at the kitchen table, having cocoa until dinner was ready. There was a knock on the door that caused Mary and Martha's hearts to almost stop. George got up and went to the door.

Two officers were there, and George's heart would have stopped if the officers weren't smiling. "Come in. It's cold out."

The two officers stepped forward, and right behind them, Tom walked in.

"Oh my God!" George exclaimed.

The women saw the officers and rushed from the kitchen, thinking it was bad news. George threw his arms around his son and let himself cry tears of joy. "I'm so..." was all he could get out before Mary and Martha put their arms around Tom.

Billy and Bobby were afraid to look in the living room, especially when they heard their grandparents and mother crying. Tears began to fall on both of their faces.

"Where are my boys?" Tom asked. When Billy and Bobby heard their father's voice, they couldn't get to him fast enough.

"You made it, Dad," Bobby said, squeezing his father.

"I knew you would," Billy said. "Now we can have our Christmas just like you promised."

George shook the officer's hands. "Thank you."

"Our pleasure, sir."

They turned to leave, and Mary stopped them. "Please, let me pack some cookies for you. You would be with your families if you didn't have to come here."

"Thank you, ma'am," they said in unison.

Mary quickly bustled to the kitchen, returning shortly with two plates of cookies. She handed them to the officers and gave them each a strong hug. "Thank you both."

After they left, everyone sat down close to Tom, just happy their Christmas wish came true.

THE END

About the Author

I am a Michigan native who has enjoyed reading and writing since 1963. Though I studied medicinal chemistry at the University of Michigan, my passion has always been writing.

I had been awarded third place for her nonfiction short story about my grandfather's escape from Poland. Later, rewrote this story and was published in the "Polish American Journal" as ""From the Pages of Grandfather's Life" and has republished it on Amazon.com as a short story.

I took creative and journalism courses to help transition to fulfill my dream of becoming a writer. I worked as an intern for Port Huron's 'The Times Herald", and also wrote, edited and did the layout or the Blue Water Multiple Sclerosis newsletters "Thumb Prints."

I run a company that helps authors get their books promoted to social media sites and four blogs, along with other sites that help promote them. It is called Owl and Pussycat Book Promotions.

You can follow Viv Drewa at the following:

Amazon: amazon.com/author/vivdrewa

Facebook: https://facebook.com/vivdrewa.author

Twitter: https://twitter.com/vivdrewa_author

Also by VIV DREWA

Please check out my other titles here:

https://www.lavishpublishing.com/authors/viv-drewa/

Also from the Lavish Family

Love on the Double Duo

L.A. Remenicky

https://www.lavishpublishing.com/authors/l-a-remenicky/

The Monroe brothers fall fast, they fall hard, and they fall forever. But the road to true love isn't always easy.

Loving Jessie's Girl – Book 1: Until AJ Monroe left Indiana after college he had always lived in his identical twin brother's shadow. He had made a life for himself in Denver, Colorado, away from Jessie, away from Indiana. But when AJ feared for his brother's safety, he left everything behind to step back into the shadow he thought he had outgrown. Finding his brother was AJ's only concern...until he met Jessie's girl.

Fiercely independent, Rina Abbot hid her true situation from everyone, including her best friend, Jessie. Out of money and unable to care for her rescue dogs she had no choice but to accept the help of the handsome stranger with a familiar face. Afraid to trust him, she tried to ignore the feelings he stirred within her as they searched for his missing brother.

But secrets never stay secrets for long.

Finally open about their feelings for each other, Rina's secrets began to wreak havoc on their lives. Would Rina's secrets force AJ to give up his dream of loving Jessie's girl?

Beyond Duty – Book 2: After serving in the Marine Corps, Jessie Monroe has finally found a life beyond war. He's focused on

being an EMT and helping his best friend rescue dogs, until he happens upon a curvy blonde stranded

with a flat tire and no jack.

On the run from her past, Dori Graham is slow to trust any man, and she tries to ignore the spark of

interest she feels for her handsome savior, but a friendship grows between them.

When Dori's past invades her new life, Jessie vows to rescue her. Saving her will take him beyond duty

and into his own personal hell. Calling upon his training as a Marine and the depth of his feelings for

Dori, Jessie will need the mental strength to battle to save her and, ultimately, save himself.

Sinister Series

A. Nicky Hjort

https://www.lavishpublishing.com/authors/nicky-hjort-1/

Thrillers that will take you to the edge and leave you breathless! Mature adult reads due to graphic sexual and violent material…

Sinister Bouquet: Awakening - Book 1: Devyn Mitchell has a choice… listen to the voice of her unborn baby – or die- again.

After a near death experience, Doctor Devyn Mitchell finds herself not only mysteriously pregnant but able to communicate with her fetus.

She has two choices: give in to total madness or surrender to her new reality, which just may be the only way she and her family will survive the obsessions of the Homeless Hunter's mind.

A true paranormal romantic thriller, A Sinister Bouquet: Awakening, the first of the Sinister Series, will take you right to the edge of what you know to be possible and then drop you in a place so dark, so terrifying, that the only passageway out is through the blinding light of awakening.

Wake up.

Open your eyes.

Finally.

We've missed you so.

Sinister Vision: Know This Much Is True – Book 2: Elise Phillips, a doctor in training, has successfully repressed her kidnapping five years prior.

The only problem is...she has six and one half days to remember every terrible detail, or a total stranger will die. But to make matters even worse, in order to save this nameless woman, Elise will have to face something that scares her even more than death–intimacy.

Another paranormal romantic thriller, A Sinister Vision: Know This Much is True, the second of the Sinister Series, will take you even further over the edge of what you know to be possible and guide you right back out through the only way left...impossible.

Wake up. Open your eyes. Accept your assignment.

...The problem is not to find the answer–but to face it.

Know this much is true.

A New Life Series

Samantha Jacobey

https://www.lavishpublishing.com/authors/samantha-jacobey/

Bikers, rockers and the FBI clash in a dark, mature adult romantic thriller – Tori Farrell will go through hell to get her new life in a completed seven book series!

To what lengths would you go to break away from a life filled with pain and suffering?

Tori Farrell has lived a dangerous life. When you grow up with a Motorcycle Gang of Mercenaries and Drug Lords like the Dragons, a normal life is more like a fairytale. For years, she accepted her dark reality, a world consisting of drugs, sex, violence and murder. In the end, she learned the most valuable lesson: survival.

After years of being ruled by the Dragons, Tori uses her skills of seduction and assassination to free herself from the grasp of the people who vowed they would never let her go. Taken in by the FBI, she fears not everything is what it seems, and soon finds herself lost in a web of lies and deceit. She thought getting away from the Dragons would put her on a path to a new and better life, but now she must face the cold hard truth... there is always a price to be paid.

www.ingramcontent.com/pod-product-compliance
Lightning Source LLC
Chambersburg PA
CBHW061254170626
46809CB00007B/2996